Have fun with Lilly
P Badilly in Costa Rica!

Sg
Jlade

The Travel Adventures of
Lilly P. Badilly
Costa Rica

Written and Illustrated by
Debbie Glade

CD Recorded at Sunflower Recording Studios, Hollywood, Florida USA

Printed in the USA

Smart Poodle Publishing
P.O. Box 817468
Hollywood, Florida 33081

To Rachel, who made Lilly come to life

To my Mother, for her courage

To all the readers out there, young and old, who possess a whacky sense of humor
and a never-ending curiosity about the world

Smart Poodle Publishing
P.O. Box 817468
Hollywood, Florida 33081
www.smartpoodlepublishing.com

The Travel Adventures of Lilly P. Badilly: Costa Rica
Written and Illustrated by Debbie Glade
ISBN 978-0-9800307-9-2

Inspiration for This Book

My fifteen-year-old daughter, Rachel, was the inspiration for the lovable child millipede, Lilly. Just like Lilly, Rachel is an avid reader, disciplined student, talented musician and a creative problem solver. It is my daughter that I generally turn to when I need advice. Her beautiful smile is a terrific comfort, and she is always a pleasure to be around.

My paternal grandparents were the inspiration for Grandma Nellie and Grandpa Willie. A bold, wig-wearing grandmother in real life, my Grandma Nellie lived to be 93. She had a great thirst for travel, adventure and fun until her last days. She spent her entire life helping others and celebrating just about everything. No matter what great challenges she faced, she remained eternally optimistic - and bossy! She was a fabulous cook, baker and hostess, an avid reader, gardener and a loyal friend. Her personality was so unique, every time I think about her, I smile.

My late Grandpa Joe, with his cautious nature, witty sense of humor and heart of gold always believed in me. Although he was afraid to try new things, Grandma Nellie was there to push him along. He never wanted to travel, but loved every trip they took together. Grandpa Joe owned a hardware store outside of Chicago, IL, and he could fix anything! He got me interested in drawing and painting. In fact, the paint brushes I used for the illustrations in the book belonged to him over 30 years ago. He is still with me every day.

For educational information about Costa Rica and for more about the creation
of this book and CD, please visit www.smartpoodlepublishing.com.

Grandpa Joe and Grandma Nellie

Costa Rica

La Cruz
Los Chiles
Tortuguero
Paos
Puerto Jesús
Alajuela
★ San José
Jabilla
Puntarenas
Puerto Limán
Drake
Nelly

Flag of Costa Rica

North and Central America

USA

Miami

Mexico

Belize

Honduras

Guatemala

Nicaragua

El Salvador

Costa Rica

Panama

"I can't wait to go on my first travel adventure!" exclaimed Lilly P. Badilly. "I know I shouldn't jump on my bed, but just thinking about a journey to the rain forest really gets me moving." Lilly began singing.

Thinking about taking a trip
Makes me want to do a flip
But I don't want to bump my head
So I'll just laugh and sing instead

Lilly P. Badilly lived in the Miami International Airport with her Grandma, Nellie O. Badilly, and her Grandpa, Willie Z. Badilly. Inside a teeny, tiny hole in a wall in Concourse A, they made themselves a cozy home. One day Grandma Nellie said, "We live in this noisy, rickety-rackety airport day in and day out. I'm tired of the same old sights, sounds and smells. It's time we climb aboard a plane to anywhere it is going. Then we can see what other creatures and yumbly, scrumbly foods the world has to offer. Plus, we can fly for free!"

"Will we find some pumpkin pie?" Lilly asked. "I just love pumpkin pie! Actually, I adore it."

"You're such a Silly Badilly, Lilly," said Grandpa Willie.

Granny wears a wig that makes her look old
But don't let that fool you 'cause she's very bold
She wants to take a journey, flying high on a jet
She's the coolest granny that you've ever met
Granny needs adventure without a delay
So if you see her coming get out of her way!

Grandpa Willie warned, "You've had a lot of buggy ideas in the past, Granny. But this time I think you've flipped your wig! Do you really think we should leave our comfy home to fly on a plane to who-knows-where?"

"Don't be such a grumpy old millipede, Willie. We're going exploring and that is that!" bossy Nellie exclaimed. "If you don't like it, you can stay home while we go without you."

Listening to Grandpa Willie made Lilly worry. She realized she might have to face some of her fears on her journey. "I wonder if I'll be afraid of the rain forest?" she asked herself. The thought of being alone in the dark made Lilly want to curl up tightly into a ball. Even worse than her fear of darkness was her fear of thunder and elevators. But what terrified Lilly the most were creepy, crawly, millipede-chomping spiders. "I don't like spiders," said Lilly. "Actually, I despise them!"

Lilly loved to read. She collected many books about animals, plants, and the environment and studied books about famous scientists and their inventions. Lilly was fascinated with music books, travel adventures, fantasies, mysteries and stories about places far, far away. "I just love to read," she exclaimed. "I love it. I still love it!"

Lilly played the piano like a pro. Her many hands and feet tickled the keys and worked the pedals. Sounds of music continually filled Lilly's head, and she liked to sing out loud. Grandpa Willie built her an itty, bitty portable piano so she could play anywhere she wanted. From classical tunes and jazzy numbers to loud rock n' roll, the Badilly home was always alive with music. "The piano makes me happier when I am sad and calmer when I am angry. And when I am cheerful, playing the piano makes me feel like I could fly!" said Lilly.

I adore tickling the keys
And I can play whatever you please
Be it smooth and slick and totally jazzy
Or rock n' rollie and really snazzy
I can play to relax you with a classical sound
Or pound on the keys 'till you hit the ground
I can make you feel a little bit creepy
Or make you happy when you feel weepy
But whatever you're feeling this much is true
Music is magic for me and you!

The day after Grandma Nellie informed the family members they were going on a journey, she sent Grandpa Willie out to check for flights. The airport monitors showed that a flight was soon leaving for San Jose, Costa Rica. Upon his return, the Badillys stuffed their backpacks for the trip. Lilly decided to bring some of her favorite books and of course, her portable piano. Grandpa Willie packed his guitar and harmonica, and Grandma Nellie packed a first aid kit. Before long, the Badilly family was on its way. Scurrying across the airport floor, the Badillys sneaked inside the briefcase of a man about to board a plane to Costa Rica.

"It's awfully dark inside this briefcase," said Lilly with fear. "I don't like it at all. Actually, I despise this darkness!" she cried.

"Here's a flashlight," whispered Grandpa Willie. "There's nothing to be afraid of now, Silly Badilly. Just think of some snazzy travel music in your head."

Lilly heard the roaring of the loud engines, and then she felt the plane taking off. She and her grandparents slid to the back of the briefcase. "Whoa!" she cried. "I can't stop rolling around. Ouch! I don't like that. Actually, I despise it!"

I hear the engines starting to roar
Soon the plane is going to soar
I'm scared of the noise, and I don't like the dark
But I'll think of eating candy and playing in a park
Can you be happy and scared at the same time?
Because that's what I am, and it isn't a crime

"We really should think about getting Lilly some singing lessons, Dear," whispered Grandma Nellie.

"Lilly sings from the heart, and that is good enough for me," Grandpa Willie said. It was quiet for a moment and then suddenly, "Ploof!" Grandpa Willie farted. Lilly laughed.

Lilly turned on the flashlight and read her Costa Rica guidebook to her grandparents. "This country in Central America is known for its beautiful volcanoes and tropical rain forest full of plants and animals. Imagine more than 800 different kinds of birds in one small country," Lilly said.

"I hope I'll see a colorful toucan, or a tiny hummingbird buzzing about," Grandma interrupted.

Lilly continued, "There are hundreds of mammals too, such as howler monkeys who make loud noises. There are anteaters that poke their long skinny noses into ant holes, and even some jaguars that speed through the forests on their strong legs. They run so fast!"

"Millipedes are just one of more than 35,000 different types of insects here," continued Lilly. "Can you believe that? Some of the more unusual critters are leaf-cutter ants, which live in huge mounds with millions of others. The butterflies are spectacular, especially the bright blue morpho. I wonder how many millipede-eating spiders there are? Yikes! I hope I never find out."

24

The plane landed smoothly in San Jose, Costa Rica. The Badillys waited in the briefcase while the passenger carried them to the baggage claim area in the airport. As they crawled out of the dark briefcase, Lilly's tummy rumbled from hunger. "I'm starving!" she declared. "I sure would enjoy a piece of scrumptious pumpkin pie with lots of fluffy whipped cream right now."

Grandpa Willie made a plan for the family to get to the Poas Volcanic National Park. He led them outside the airport to secretly board a colorful city bus. From the back window, they admired the sights of the city while filling their bellies with a mushy, squishy banana someone left behind. Old Grandpa Willie farted again. "Ploof!"

"Oops, must have been the overripe banana," he whispered.

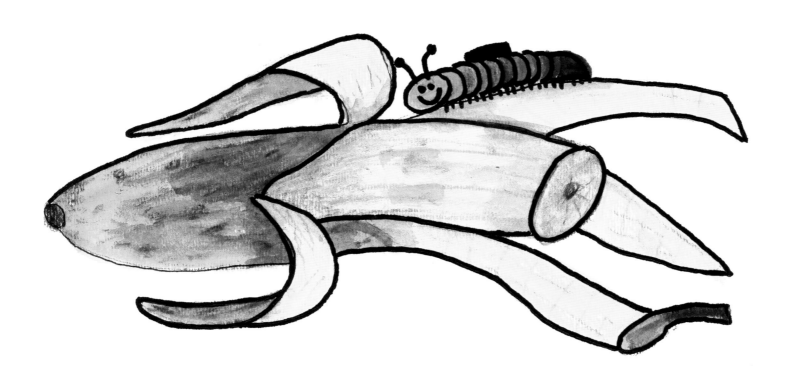

Lilly heard the friendly people on the bus speaking beautiful Spanish, like many people did at the Miami Airport. But she could not understand what they were saying.

The bus passed through the crowded city streets and stopped at the outdoor San Jose Vegetable Market. Lilly's eyes opened wide with amazement. She had never seen so many people in one place. She even saw a colorful hand-painted ox cart, known as a carreta. It was the most beautiful object she had ever seen. "Carts like this were made centuries ago to help farmers carry their fruits and vegetables as they harvested the fields," Lilly told her grandparents.

"Oh please, please, Grandma Nellie, can we get off this bus and eat? Pleeeaase!!" begged Lilly. "I love this kind of food. I really love it."

"Sorry, Lilly, but we must stay on the bus to get to the rain forest," replied Grandma Nellie.

At the Poas Volcanic National Park, huge trees shaded the forest. The sounds of birds whistling loud tunes and the chirping of insects filled the humid air. A beautiful rain forest tune danced in Lilly's mind. As she crawled into the monstrous forest, she experienced both excitement and anxiety at the same time; her four biggest fears were always on her mind.

I'm on my journey
I'm off to explore
I don't know what I'll find
On that big forest floor
My grandparents will protect me
I won't think of my fears
We'll have a fun adventure
I'll cherish for years

"Let's go down this path," said Grandpa Willie. "We need to find a good, safe place to sleep tonight while it's still light outside. Then we can explore the volcano tomorrow. I am afraid it looks like it's going to storm."

Deep inside the forest, the wind hissed, and the sky rumbled. Rain pounded down in big splish-splashing drops. "I don't like the sound of this storm," declared Grandpa Willie.

Lilly trembled. "I don't like thunder and lightning. Actually, I despise them!" she cried.

Grandpa Willie found a hole in a huge rock for the family to crawl into. "We'll stay safe and dry in here," he said. Grandma Nellie pulled a crisp, dead leaf inside the rock. The Badillys munched on something crunchy while drinking droplets of water from the top.

"I don't think this travel adventure was such a good idea," said Lilly. "I wish I were in my own cozy bed right now."

"Oh, Lilly, you simply cannot see the world from your room, Dear. Don't worry. We're safe in here," assured Grandma Nellie.

Lilly tried not to be afraid, but lightning zapped the sky and thunder rolled louder and louder, getting closer and closer. The massive drops of rain thumped down, passing by the opening in the rock and splashing on the ground. The sounds created a catchy repetitive tune Lilly hummed. "Ta-dum, whoosh! ta-dum, whoosh! ta-dum..."

Suddenly Lilly hollered, "Look! There's a rhinoceros beetle over there on his back. He's injured and cannot move. We've got to help him, Grandpa Willie! He's getting pounded by the rain."

Grandpa Willie bravely rushed to approach the beetle. "Be careful, Willie!" yelled Grandma Nellie from inside the rock.

"I see you are injured, Mr. Beetle," said Grandpa Willie. "Let me help you move to a safe, dry place."

"You are so kind," replied the beetle. "I think I sprained one of my six ankles, particularly my hind. You see rhino beetles can carry 850 times their weight on their backs. I tried to carry too much, but I couldn't make it with that many snacks."

Lilly and Nellie saw Grandpa Willie struggling to help the beetle out of the storm, so they ran out to assist. All three millipedes pushed and shoved and nudged and heaved until the beetle turned over, dumping his heavy load on the wet ground.

"Thank you for saving me. How wonderful it is to be free. I thought there was one millipede, but now I see three. Can you guess my name? Can you play the fiddle? If you can make a rhyme you'd know that my name is - - -"

"Riddle," said Lilly, with a grin on her face.

Just as Riddle stood up, a huge, ogre-faced spider, hanging by her silky thread, suddenly dropped from a tree. She threw her silk web net over the insects and scooped them high up in the air.

Lilly thought to herself, "I don't like this. Actually, I despise it! Not only am I terrified of millipede-eating spiders, thunderstorms and darkness, I'm also frightened of elevators, and being in this net is just like getting stuck in an elevator. I want to go home right now!"

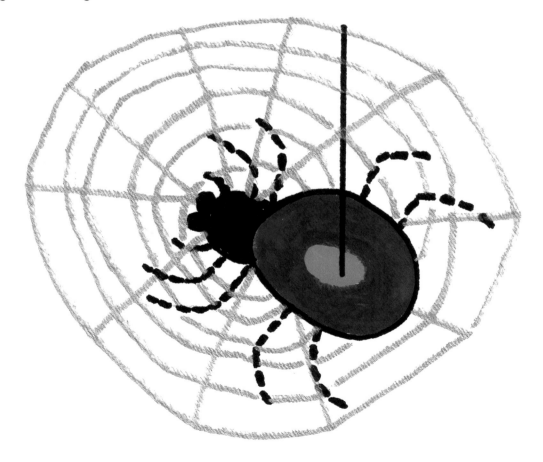

When the Badillys reached the spider's destination deep inside the tall oak tree, they gasped. The branches were full of scores of other webs that trapped some of the most unusual insects they had ever seen.

"Some of the critters in those webs are our enemies too. If they can get to us, what do you think they'll do?" cried Riddle. "But I guess that does not matter now, because we'll all be eaten by that nasty spider anyhow."

"You can count on that," claimed the cruel spider. "In a few days I will feast on you after I've eaten all these other appetizing creatures." Then the spider lowered herself back to the ground to search for more victims.

I can't believe this is happening
I can't believe it's true
I know I should not panic
But what else can I do?

Lilly cried from worry and panic. She tried to relax by looking over at all the other colorful, fascinating creatures in the webs. But the sight of them trapped in net bundles made her feel even worse.

Grandma Nellie turned her head for a bird's-eye view of the forest. "Look! There's the Poas Volcano in the distance. It's more amazing than I ever imagined!" she exclaimed.

"Oh, it is spectacular," said Grandpa Willie. "But don't you think we better figure out how to get out of this trap instead of admiring that volcano?"

Grandpa Willie's nerves made him start farting again. "Ploof!" But everyone was too scared to laugh.

"Let us get some sleep now that it is getting dark," whispered Riddle. "That spider will not eat us at night in the park. Rather she will wait until the sun comes up and hears the singing of the lark."

Lilly tried, but she could not sleep one wink for two whole nights.

As the sun came up on the third day, a morpho butterfly, named Imago, mumbled, "We've been trapped for many days, and I'm afraid we'll never get out. I am so hungry and weak."

"Let's not panic," declared Grandpa Willie. "We can all help each other. And let's agree now there will be no fighting amongst us."

"We agree," said all the prisoners.

Despite panicking about the spider's return, Lilly created inspiring music in her head. She told herself, "If I concentrate on my fears, we'll never get out of here alive. I've got to be strong!"

Lilly sat quietly and thought hard for a long time. After a while she figured out how to trick that creepy spider and help all the prisoners escape alive from the tree. Lilly turned to Grandpa Willie and whispered her secret plan. They both took out their musical instruments and began to play. Just then that nasty spider pulled herself back up into the tree.

Lilly softly played soothing piano music while Grandpa strummed along on the guitar. All the while, he managed to whisper the escape plan to Grandma Nellie and Riddle.

"What is that noise I hear?" the spider demanded to know.

"That's piano music I am playing," explained Lilly. "And he's playing the guitar. Do you like it?" she asked.

"Well I wouldn't say I like anything – that is – other than eating crunchy insects like you," the spider laughed. But Lilly kept playing. And the spider settled down to rest a bit while all the insects listened with fascination. Many had never heard music before.

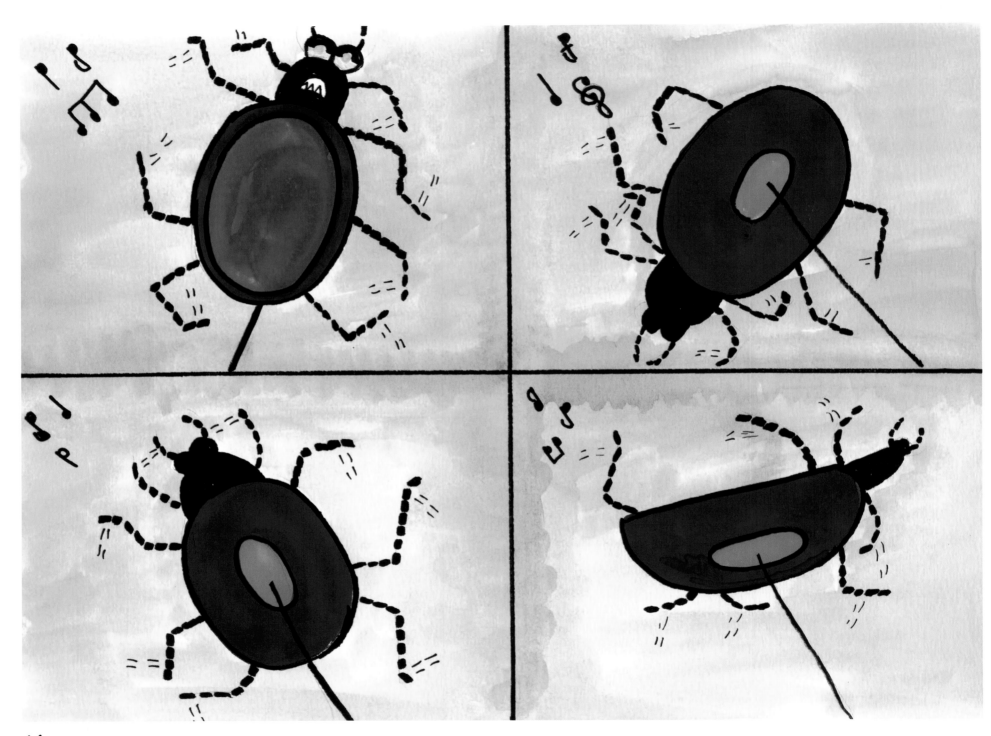

"What's your name?" Lilly asked the spider.
"Ruth," replied the grumpy spider, "Ruth Less. Why do you want to know?"

I met a spider named Ruth Less
Unfortunately for us she wasn't toothless
She pulled us into her web of a net
And she would not let us forget
She was hungry and she was mean
And she was the cruelest spider ever seen . . .

Ruth raised herself up in the air from her web string, twirling and dancing.
"I love that music! Play more!" she demanded.

I love to dance and hop and sing
And you know what is the craziest thing?
When I move, and when I hop
It seems as though I can never stop!
I jump real high and twist real low
I move so fast, and I sing real slow
But no matter how long I sing and dance
It seems to put me in a trance
Now I feel peaceful, now I am sleepy
Now I must rest, before I feel weepy. . .
Ruth Less
Not toothless
Web of a net
Not let us forget

While Ruth danced, Riddle whispered the details of Lilly's escape plan to the nearby prisoners. Riddle used his long horn to drill a hole in the web and pull a sharp branch off from the tree. Then he poked the stick through the web where Imago, the butterfly, was trapped. That loosened the seal of Imago's web. Then Imago poked the stick through another web, and so on. Before long, each of the web nets had openings, and the branch dropped to the ground. Ruth was so busy dancing, she never noticed that the insects all had escape holes in their webs. "I love to dance, dance, dance!" Ruth shouted.

Just as planned, Ruth wore herself out from dancing and fell asleep. Deeper and deeper she slept as all the once-trapped insects scrambled down the tree. Grandpa Willie wrapped webbing tightly around Ruth and twisted it closed, so she could not recapture them when she awoke. "Hurry," Grandpa Willie whispered, "Let's get out of here before Ruth wakes up!" The Badilly family, along with Riddle, quickly packed up their musical instruments, zipped up their backpacks, and they too climbed down the tree to safety.

At the bottom of the tree, the freed insects celebrated their escape and thanked Lilly for her brilliant plan. A morpho butterfly named Metta, a dragonfly named Chopper and a moth named Wooly asked Lilly, Nellie and Willie if they'd like a ride over the Poas Volcano. "Can we, Grandma? Can we?" begged Lilly. "I've always wanted to be able to fly. Oh please, Grandma!"

"I don't think that it would be safe," stated Grandpa Willie.

"Nonsense." Grandma said. "This is the only way we will have time to truly see the rainforest and volcano before catching our plane back home."

The Badillys each said goodbye to their new friend, Riddle. With tears in his eyes Riddle riddled, "Who is kind and generous and saved my life? I'll answer that myself - a Silly Badilly, a Grandpa and his wife."

Each of the Badillys climbed aboard one of the flying insects and held on tight.

From high in the sky the Badillys looked at the rain forest and listened to the soothing sound of the rushing wind. Lilly could not believe her eyes. "Costa Rica is so beautiful from up here. I have never seen so many trees. And look, Grandpa Willie, there's the central crater of the Poas volcano."

Grandpa Willie said, "I am so proud of you, Lilly. You bravely worked through your fears, and your music saved us all. You are a true hero."

"Thanks, Grandpa," replied Lilly. "That was the best trip anyone could ever take. Maybe I won't be as scared of the things I'm scared of any more."

"Maybe you won't," said Grandpa. "Though it is perfectly normal for everyone – even adults - to be afraid sometimes."

Metta, Chopper and Wooly flew the Badilly family all the way to the San Jose Airport, so they could catch a plane ride back home to Miami. "We sure do appreciate that unforgettable ride," said Grandpa Willie as he thanked the graceful flyers for their transportation services.

"It's the least we could do," said Chopper, "After all, you saved us from Ruth Less!"

"Come and visit us sometime in Miami," insisted Grandma Nellie, before they parted ways.

Once inside the airport, the Badillys crawled inside a woman's duffle bag to board Flight 22 back to the Miami International Airport. "I am really tired, Grandma," Lilly said with a sigh.

"Me too," Grandma Nellie said.

"Me three, Silly Badilly," Grandpa Willie said.

And the three Badillys curled up inside the cozy duffle bag atop the fluffy clothes and slept all the way home.

I went to the rain forest
To see the plants
Hear the birds
To talk to the ants
I almost got eaten
By a spider named Ruth
And when she awoke
She learned the truth
Being selfish and mean
Can get you into trouble
But being clever and smart
Will earn you double
I'm not as afraid
Of thunder and dark
And elevators and spiders
Who roam in the park
I'm only scared a little
And that is enough
My name is Lilly
And I'm really tough!

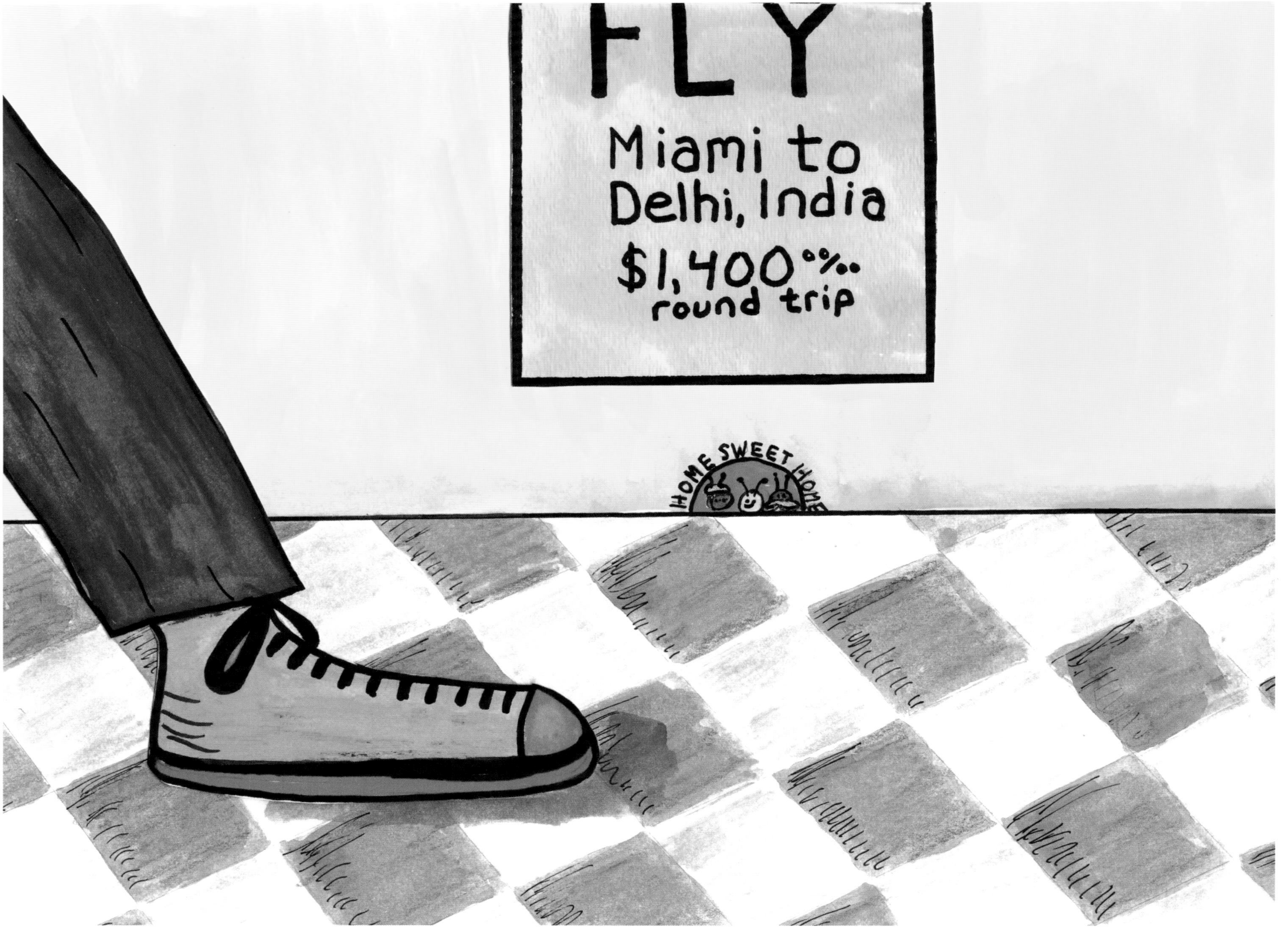
FLY
Miami to
Delhi, India
$1,400
round trip
HOME SWEET HOME

Before long the Badillys were back inside their home in a teeny, tiny hole in a wall in Concourse A of the Miami International Airport. Grandma Nellie made Lilly her favorite fluffy pumpkin pie with whipped cream. And there went Grandpa Willie again, farting up a storm. "Ploof!"

"I love Costa Rica,
I really love it!"

About the Author

Author and illustrator, Debbie Glade, worked as a researcher and travel writer for the cruise-line industry for many years. She combined this background with her artistic and voice talents to create a book that would not only entertain children but also teach them about geography and nature – and about themselves. She holds a Bachelor's degree in Creative Writing from Florida State University. Mrs. Glade lives in South Florida with her husband, daughter and standard poodle, along with a whole lot of books.